W9-BHU-240

THE WILLOW PATTERN

Have you ever seen
the willow pattern plate?
It is white with a blue
design that tells a story.
Painted into the plate
is a beautiful Chinese fairy tale.

Contents

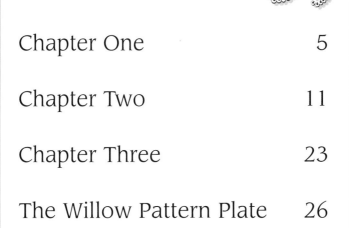

Chapter One

Long, long ago, in old China, there lived a powerful elder called a mandarin. His clothes were of the finest embroidered silk. The rings on his fingers were dazzling in the sunlight. And his name was T'so Ling. He loved his daughter more than anything in the world. Her skin was as pale as a white magnolia flower. Her hair was as black as the night sky. And her name was Koong-se. They lived in a fine house by a river, which was guarded by a large willow tree. Its graceful limbs bowed to the mandarin and his beautiful daughter.

In one corner of the mandarin's garden was a summer house. There Koong-se spent her days embroidering silk and listening to her bird sing in its bamboo cage. Her kind servant watched over Koong-se with a smile.

One day, a new clerk came to work for the mandarin. His tall body was as willowy as the tree that grew by the river. His eyes were soft and full of dreams. He was a poet. And his name was Chang. When he saw Koong-se, he fell in love with her at once. He wrote beautiful poems, telling Koong-se of his love for her. The two fell deeply in love.

With the help of Koong-se's faithful servant, the young couple met secretly every evening in the summer house. They would talk together, and Chang would read his poems.

As Chang sat at Koong-se's feet reading poetry in the summer house one evening, the door burst open.

"What is the meaning of this?"

It was the mandarin. His eyes flashed in anger. Chang stood up and bowed deeply.

"I am so sorry, Great T'so Ling. This will never happen again!"

"No, it will not!" roared the mandarin. "You will leave my house immediately. If you ever come back, I will cut out your tongue – so you will never speak to my daughter again!"

Chang hurried out in shame.

Then the mandarin turned to the servant who was trembling in terror.

"Why do you allow a common clerk to sit with my beautiful daughter?" he demanded.

The servant bowed her head and said, "I'm sorry, oh Great T'so Ling."

"And so you shall be!" the mandarin roared. "I banish you from my household."

Then he looked at his daughter.

"It is time I found you a suitable husband! Until then, you will not leave the grounds of my house!"

Koong-se stared at her father in dismay.

Chapter Two

True to his word, T'so Ling made arrangements for his daughter to marry a wealthy and important man called a ta-jin. The ta-jin was cold and cruel. And he was old.

There was now a high fence surrounding the mandarin's house on one side with the river on the other. The broken-hearted Koong-se sat miserably by the willow tree, gazing into the water. Suddenly she spied a tiny boat made out of half a coconut shell. It sailed past in the murky water.

"What a lovely little boat!" she said and scooped it up.

Inside was a piece of rice paper – it was a message from Chang!

"Your beauty is as bright as a star, and I worship you still from afar!"

She held it close to her heart. And when her grumpy new servant was not looking, she wrote her own message.

"I am to marry the ta-jin when the peach trees bloom.
Help me!"

She placed the message inside the tiny coconut boat and pushed it off into the water.

The day of the wedding grew near. Presents arrived from far and wide. They glittered and shone, but they brought no happiness to poor Koong-se. She had not heard back from her beloved Chang. And soon she would be married to a cruel man whom she did not love. Koong-se felt like a bird caught in a net, powerless to escape her fate.

The ta-jin presented her with a precious gift. It was a decorated box full of glittering jewels. She smiled weakly, but when he was gone, tears slid down her satin-smooth skin.

On the eve of her wedding there were great celebrations. The house was filled with the sounds of festivity and feasting. Koong-se sat quietly in her room and wept.

14

Then, into the garden came a very strange-looking guest. His clothes were not as fine as those of the others, and his face was hidden. No one noticed as he silently sneaked over to the house. Koong-se looked up and saw a figure creeping up to her room. It was Chang!

"You've come for me!" she cried.

"I could never let you marry the cruel ta-jin!" said Chang.

Koong-se threw her arms around him and hugged him tightly.

"Oh, Chang – let's get away!"

Just then, the grumpy servant came in.

"Who is this?" she demanded.

"Koong-se, we must run!" cried Chang.

He grabbed her by the hand, and they ran past the guests who had gathered around. Koong-se quickly snatched up her box of jewels.

The servant started shouting for help, and all eyes turned to the fleeing couple.

The mandarin raced after them. He followed Chang and Koong-se over the bridge, but he couldn't keep up. The young couple soon left him behind.

The ta-jin was very angry that his bride had escaped, taking his jewels with her. He sent out soldiers to look for her and pledged that Koong-se must be returned to him.

Chang and Koong-se found shelter at the house of Koong-se's faithful servant and friend. There they were married and lived in secrecy, leaving the house only after nightfall.

One evening a soldier came to the little house and demanded to search for the couple.

"If they are hidden here, they will not escape. There are guards in the street, and at the back of the house there is only the river."

Although the servant was in great danger, she did not want to betray her friends. She kept talking to the soldier while Koong-se and Chang escaped out a window and headed down the river in a boat.

Chapter Three

The little boat sailed on down the fast-flowing river for several days. One morning it drifted onto land.

"It's an island!" said Chang. "Let us make this our home!"

And that is what they did. They sold the jewels in a nearby town and, with the money they made, bought the island. Together they built a small house and worked the land until the finest vegetables grew.

They were very happy until one terrible day the cruel ta-jin found out where they lived.

"I will teach them to dare cross me!" he roared. And he sent his army to the island.

There were too many soldiers for the brave Chang. And soon the little house where he and Koong-se had spent many happy hours was ablaze with fire.

But that was not the end of the story. Out of the flames flew two doves. Koong-se and Chang were transformed into immortal love birds, and they flew high in the sky, where the cruel ta-jin could never harm them again.

THE WILLOW PATTERN PLATE

The willow pattern design has been around for more than two hundred years. Traditionally, the pattern was painted into the plate with a metal oxide paint. Today, transfers can be used to create the same effect.

The story begins with the process of clay to plate.

Liquid earthenware clay, called "slip," is poured into a plaster-of-paris mold. The mold absorbs moisture from the clay. It takes about two hours for the clay to set.

When the plate is leather-hard, it is trimmed and removed from the mold. At this stage, the clay is called "greenware" and is very fragile.

When the greenware is completely dry, bumps and imperfections are removed with a special knife. This is called "fettling."

The plate is now ready for its first firing. It is baked in a kiln at 1976°F for eight hours, and then left to cool for sixteen hours before it can be removed.

The plate is now brittle and firm and is called "bisque." Glaze, a liquid form of glass, is applied to the plate to seal it and make it waterproof.

After it has been returned to the kiln and fired again, the plate has a shiny finish. It is now ready for the transfer.

A special transfer that has been printed with china paint is soaked in warm water and applied to the plate. Any bubbles are smoothed out with a small sponge.

The plate is fired again to 1472°F. At this temperature, the glaze starts to soften and the colors of the china paint are melted in and become part of the plate.

And that is how a willow pattern plate is made.

From the Author

As a child, I remember seeing the willow pattern plate, but I never realized until I was older that it told a story.

I run a children's theater where we perform traditional fairy tales on stage. One day, I thought about presenting *The Willow Pattern* as a play. I was fascinated with the idea of having all the scenery and costumes in blue and white.

As yet, I still haven't staged *The Willow Pattern* – but you could!

Carol Krueger

From the Illustrator

I found that my illustrations for *The Willow Pattern* flowed quite naturally, probably because Chinese culture has always been a significant part of my life. As a child, I took my  Chinese surroundings for granted and often wished for a true Western-style home complete with bunks and a swimming pool.

Gradually, I grew to love my parents' treasures of Chinese vases, necklaces, and carvings. Today, antique jugs and bowls from my father's village are some of my most prized possessions.

Marie Low

© Text by **Carol Krueger**
© Illustrations by **Marie Low**
Edited by **Frances Bacon**
Designed by **Nicola Evans**

© 1999 Shortland Publications, Inc.
All rights reserved. No part of this publication may be reproduced or
transmitted in any form or by any means, electronic or mechanical, including
photocopying, recording, taping, or any information storage and retrieval
system, without permission in writing from the publisher.

04 03 02 01 00
10 9 8 7 6 5 4 3 2

Distributed in the United States by
   RIGBY
   a division of Reed Elsevier Inc.
   P.O. Box 797
   Crystal Lake, IL 60039-0797

Printed in Hong Kong.
ISBN: 0-7699-0417-3